The Experiment

Mark Ravenhill

A SAMUEL FRENCH ACTING EDITION

SAMUEL FRENCH

FOUNDED 1830

SAMUELFRENCH.COM
SAMUELFRENCH-LONDON.CO.UK

MUSIC USE NOTE

Licensees are solely responsible for obtaining formal written permission from copyright owners to use copyrighted music in the performance of this play and are strongly cautioned to do so. If no such permission is obtained by the licensee, then the licensee must use only original music that the licensee owns and controls. Licensees are solely responsible and liable for all music clearances and shall indemnify the copyright owners of the play(s) and their licensing agent, Samuel French, against any costs, expenses, losses and liabilities arising from the use of music by licensees. Please contact the appropriate music licensing authority in your territory for the rights to any incidental music.

IMPORTANT BILLING AND CREDIT REQUIREMENTS

If you have obtained performance rights to this title, please refer to your licensing agreement for important billing and credit requirements.

1.

Please god: help me to remember.

This was – I suppose – a long time ago.

And I remember I lived in a modest house with my partner.

And I think maybe – your face – you were one of our neighbours.

And we were very happy in that big old house. Very.

Because we had children. One of each. A perfect pair. A very special unique wonderful child.

And I remember – yes – it was us – it was…in our great big manor house…one time…it was… I remember…

We ran the tests on the children.

Because you see we sort of knew that one day one of the children would grow up to have an incurable disease – an, as yet, incurable disease – so what we – we – my partner decided and I followed – we decided together – what we decided to do was to experiment on the children. Because then we'd have the cure when the time came. We'd find the cure for the child's later ailment.

So we were – if I remember – very thorough about this, very organised. Mostly organised. An organised chaos.

And we would infect the child, the children with little drops of viruses or inject little cells of cancers and we – you know through the bars of the cage

The cage was in a film. I saw the cage in a film – a documentary or a horror

Or there was a cage in the fairy story my grandmother told me on the train journey that time to…to…

So there wasn't maybe there wasn't – no cage.

Because the child had a lovely room. The best room in that cramped little house. Stars that glowed on the ceiling, wallpaper of princesses, a rug with a map of an imaginary world

But because my partner had an incurable illness – it wasn't curable at that time – that's when my partner decided to run the tests on the children

My partner told me on a rainy hot winter night afternoon as we made breakfast lying on the sundeck and he was over there and my partner told me

I have an incurable illness and what we must do is run tests on the children so that we can find the new medicine to save me

And I can't remember I…

Was totally opposed

I understood immediately

I was dumbstruck, didn't know what to do

This didn't happen to me, this happened to another person. Another person living with another partner in another

This happened to you

This happened to a person I saw in a documentary once

So I went along with it

I remember I strapped the child to the bed

I was very kind, I was soothing, I loved my child but I loved my partner, we had to find a cure

What you have to do to get through something like that when you know it's for the greater good what you do is you numb your feelings – you cut out your heart, you cut it…

I remember nothing about the tests beginning.

Just suddenly you're there and your partner has strapped the child to the bed and is injecting the child with tiny drops of viruses and cancers

And I can't remember anything about it

I remember the children slept through the worst of it

I was sleeping all the time

And I remember waking up and I said to my partner: the most awful thing is happening next door. The couple next door are experimenting on their children so that they can find a cure.

And my partner said: That sort of thing goes on of course I know it, it goes on but a long way a long time ago

But I was so sure and I took a – I think if I remember – it was the new video camera and I climbed over the fence and into our neighbour's garden

I was you know – it was probably after two three six months years of this

After a while you – you imagine this was you – imagine you're me – after a while you just have to know if this is a real thing you have to have something on record

So I was I remember the Christmas lights were still up and in the baking heat I'm making my way up the stairs in that big house

It was the shed door, I think I remember the child's voice from behind the

Father, father, the needle is sharp

Mother, mother, cut out your heart

Which I remember in verse which can't be, that must be…there wasn't any…there can't have been…but here in my head verse

Father, father, cut out the heart

Mother, mother the needle is...

And I pushed pulled open the door swung open and through the eye of the camera I saw my partner neighbour injecting the child strapped to the bed and sleeping

And I remember calling out I:

Dear god, what is this? Has it come to this? Are we animals? We who are God's creation? We are so close to the angels? We who are reason and imagination? Is this what we're doing with all that god has given us? These tests? These experiments?

I wish I'd said that. When I go back in my head, when I tell the story to myself or to you that's what I wish I'd 'we who are God's creation' I wish those words

But I remember I...

I just remember screaming CUNT CUNT CUNT CUNT CUNT over and over and

Because of course – I didn't – that's right – I remember now, I remember, the order was muddled, it didn't happen

We lived in a modest manor house long ago and I suppose I had my suspicions because why else – I can't think of any other reason why I'd be pushing open the door with the video camera in my time but I didn't

Yes I didn't know anything about the – that's it I didn't know anything about the experiments or the reasons for the experiments until then

I knew nothing at all

I knew nothing and that's why I reacted so: CUNT

And that's when my partner sat me down on the lounger standing there with the vodka in my hand the tea was cold and the weather was hot rain and my partner explained to me

Next door they have an as yet incurable disease so what we must do is experiment on your child so that we can find a cure. Our children may suffer a little, I grant you, but it will find a cure for the disease next door

And that's when I remember my partner telling me because I still had the video camera in my hand because this must have been before the video camera was stolen but that was another video camera

And so I remember I agreed to the experiments

That's how my partner made me agree to the experiments

There once was a person who agreed to experiments on children if it would find a cure

And I remember my neighbour was angry – was it you? – maybe it was you? – you were sarcastic mocking teasing furious understanding

Your partner makes his money because he has shares in a company that experiments on children

And I remember I told you: To prevent an incurable disease.

And you I remember you backed off away then.

And this child is. Look at this child. This child is so damaged. It has no memory. There is no past or future for this child. This child has no moral sense. This child could not tell you: this is right, this is wrong. This child has no empathy: this child cannot feel anything that others feel. Can we really say that it is wrong to experiment on this child? I would not call this child an animal because – quite honestly – that would be degrading to the animal.

2.

I'm in the room

The room is squalid

Pizza box beer cans

And I'm looking at my twin brother

And his skin is hard and dry, red, blistered. It's over his hands, starting to cover his face

And I'm looking at him sitting on the bed

And I think that he hates me for my clothes and my smooth skin

And my twin asks me:

'Don't you remember? Don't you remember what they did to us?'

'How he woke us up at night and he put on our pyjamas and he took us down the stairs

Don't you remember that?'

Maybe

'And how they took us to the cupboard under the stairs

And how dark it was under the stairs

And how you could hear the other children crying in there too'

Possibly

'And how the train pulled in under the stairs

And how we all got into the train

And how it went to the mountains

And how he liked us because we were twins

Do you remember?'

A little bit

'And we never saw the other children again

They were washed away

But he took us into his special room

And he did the experiments on us

Do you remember that?'

I'm not sure

'And one day he cried

Cried so much and he said:

'Humanity has ended

Soon the last human will go

But that's alright

Because I'm going to make new humans

You see that's why I'm doing the experiments on you

So that when the time comes there'll be a new human race

And they'll all be made from your cells

If only I can get the experiment right

Do you see?'

And he stopped crying

And there was a big smile on his face

Do you remember that? You must – big smile on his face – remember that?'

And I said :

No

None of that happened

You need help

You need to be sorted

It didn't happen

Humanity didn't die

Open the curtains

Look outside

There's a whole human race out there

They're not us

They weren't made in a room by experimenting on us

Each one is unique and individual and –

Why did you make that up?

And my twin says to me:

'You're the one who makes things up. I'm the one who tells the truth'

You're the one who makes things up. I'm the one who tells the truth.

3.

And I remember after three ten years the child grew too big for that room for the shed for the I remember the children growing absolutely big and enormous.

And I said to my partner : The experiments on the children have ended.

And it was my partner who told me: The experiments on the children have ended.

We saw it – I'm pretty sure – on the news first: The experiments on the children have ended.

Somewhere else somebody else had found a cure by experimenting on…

I forget.

Don't remember.

I remember so clearly rushing up the grand stairs in the grand hall of the manor house –

Only of course they weren't there at the time –

I ran into my partner's office in the City and I said:

'They've found we've discovered there's a cure antidote and the children's neighbour's lives is saved – you are going to live my darling – and here's the first pill'

And I remember thinking that you were going to live forever

4.

The other day, it had been a beautiful day

We'd been up to the shopping centre where we'd been
celebrating another victory

And we got the bus home

And it was so lovely

Because everybody was so happy about the victory

And they were all smiling and congratulating each
other

And a big black lady pulled me into her bosom and
just held me and said:

'Another victory praise be praise be'

And we got home

And I was making us a drink to have on the balcony

When my partner said:

'I saw them again'

I wanted to hit my partner and tell my partner to shut
it

But I'm better educated than that so I said:

'Yes?'

And my partner said:

'The two little boys

It was the noise at first

Because they were calling out

'Father father the needle is sharp'

But then I saw them at the end of the bed

Two bodies but joined here and here

Two but one

And they were naked

And there were injection marks all over here

And little cuts all over here

And their eyes

And their teeth

Had been pulled and –

Is this how they made us? Is this who we are?

Did they do these tests, these experiments so we can –?

What if we're not humans

None of us are real humans anymore

But we're all just made by the man who cut at those boys in a shed in the…'

And I said

'Look the sun is setting

It's very beautiful

And this drink tastes lovely

So let's just… Yes?'

I won't be with this partner

Nothing lasts forever

But as long as we don't talk about the experiments

We'll have a few years

And that's lovely.